Nicholas Nosh, the littlest pirate in the world, wasn't allowed to go to sea.

'You're too small,' said his dad.

'When you're bigger you can go,' said his mum.

His older brother and sister just laughed. They all boarded their ship, the *Pig's Breakfast*.

'Be good,' shouted his dad.

'Eat your broccoli,' said his mum.

'Don't touch our stuff!' yelled his brother and sister.

And they sailed away to capture treasure.

Nicholas was left at home with his babysitter, Gretta.
She was so tall that Nicholas barely reached her knees.

Sometimes Nicholas climbed up her long, black plaits.
It was like climbing the ropes on a ship.

Gretta loved to cook, especially puddings and sweets.
But sometimes her cooking was a disaster.

the Littlest Pirate

Sherryl Clark

illustrated by Tom Jellett

For Mia and Dion - SC

For Frank and Tony - TJ

Published by
HAPPY CAT BOOKS
An imprint of Catnip Publishing Ltd
14 Greville Street
London EC1N 8SB

This edition first published 2009
1 3 5 7 9 10 8 6 4 2

First published by Penguin Group (Australia), 2008

Text copyright © Sherryl Clark, 2008
Illustrations copyright © Tom Jellett, 2008

The moral right of the author/illustrator has been asserted

A CIP catalogue record for this book is available from the British Library

ISBN 978-1-905117-88-8

Printed in China

www.catnippublishing.co.uk

The spare pirate crew left behind didn't care. They ate all of Gretta's food and grew very fat and lazy. They were supposed to be mending the spare ship, the *Golden Heart*. It had big worm holes in the hull.

Nicholas was bored. He'd practised with his cutlass and axe, and read his favourite book, *The Biggest, Nastiest Pirates of all Time*. He'd played with all the treasure in the treasure room, but it wasn't the same as capturing it.

He was so bored that he decided to run away and join another pirate ship. 'I'll show them,' he said.

Nicholas packed his cutlass and axe, and pulled on his best leather boots. Then he put on his pirate hat and set off over the hills.

In the next town, Nicholas found lots of ships tied up along the waterfront. In front of one ship was a sign that read:

Captain Scab was sitting on a hatch cover, mending a sail. His trousers were worn and his boots had no laces. Old cannonballs and bones littered the deck.

'I want to be a pirate on your ship,' Nicholas said.

Captain Scab frowned at him. 'You don't look big enough.'

'I'm very good at sword fighting,' said Nicholas.

'Can you fire a musket or a cannon?' asked Captain Scab.

'Er . . . no,' said Nicholas. 'But I'm great at swabbing decks and I can climb to the top of any mast.'

'Hmm,' Captain Scab growled. 'I suppose I could give you a go.'

Just then Gretta came running along the wharf. 'Nicholas!
Nicholas!' she called.

Nicholas tried to hide behind Captain Scab, but it was
too late. Gretta had seen him.

'Nicholas!' Gretta puffed. 'You have to come home. Red Beard has captured your mother and father and brother and sister. I have a ransom note. Red Beard wants all of the treasure.'

'He can't leave yet,' said Captain Scab. 'I've got lots of rats for him to catch.'

'Sorry,' said Nicholas quickly. 'I have to save my family. Bye.'

Back at the cove lay the spare pirate ship, the *Golden Heart*. The spare pirate crew were busy loading cannonballs and old muskets on board.

'I'll pack the food,' said Gretta.

'I'll get a map and a compass,' said Nicholas.

Off they set to search for Red Beard. A strong wind filled the sails, and the *Golden Heart* sped across the water. Nicholas stood at the wheel, steering west.

'Excuse me, Captain,' said a pirate. His feet were dripping wet. 'There's water in the hold.'

'Take the wheel,' Nicholas said. He went below to investigate.

Oh no! The lazy pirates had done a very bad job of mending the worm holes. The ship was still leaking. Water was sloshing everywhere.

Nicholas raced up to the galley, where Gretta was stirring toffee in a big pot.

'What can we do?' he said. 'We're sinking, and there's no tar left to fill the leaks.'

'What about this toffee?' said Gretta. 'I think it will set.'

The toffee was bubbling and thick. Nicholas carried some below. He ordered the pirates to bail out the water, then he quickly spooned toffee into each hole. The toffee set hard and fast, and the leaking stopped.

'Yay!' cheered the crew. Nicholas was turning out to be a very clever captain.

The *Golden Heart* caught up with Red Beard's ship the next morning. The *Black Bog* was huge. It had four masts and forty cannons. It flew a black flag with a red spider on it.

Through his spyglass, Nicholas could see his mum and dad and brother and sister. They sat on the foredeck, tied together with rope. Red Beard stood over them. He was the biggest pirate Nicholas had ever seen. Four pistols hung from his belt. Spiders crawled in his long, red beard.

Nicholas shivered. He felt very little. 'We need to fire our cannons and bring down the masts,' he said, trying to be brave. 'Then we have to board and take the ship.'

But when he checked the cannonballs, he discovered that the lazy pirates had packed all the wrong shapes and sizes. None of them would fit.

Nicholas went to the galley. Gretta stood by the stove, frowning into a large pot. There were rows of bowls lined up on the table, filled with horrible yellow sticky stuff.

'What are you cooking?' Nicholas asked.

'Caramel puddings. Some are too heavy, some are too runny. I don't know where I went wrong.'

As he stared at the puddings, Nicholas had a wonderful idea. 'Can I have these?' he asked.

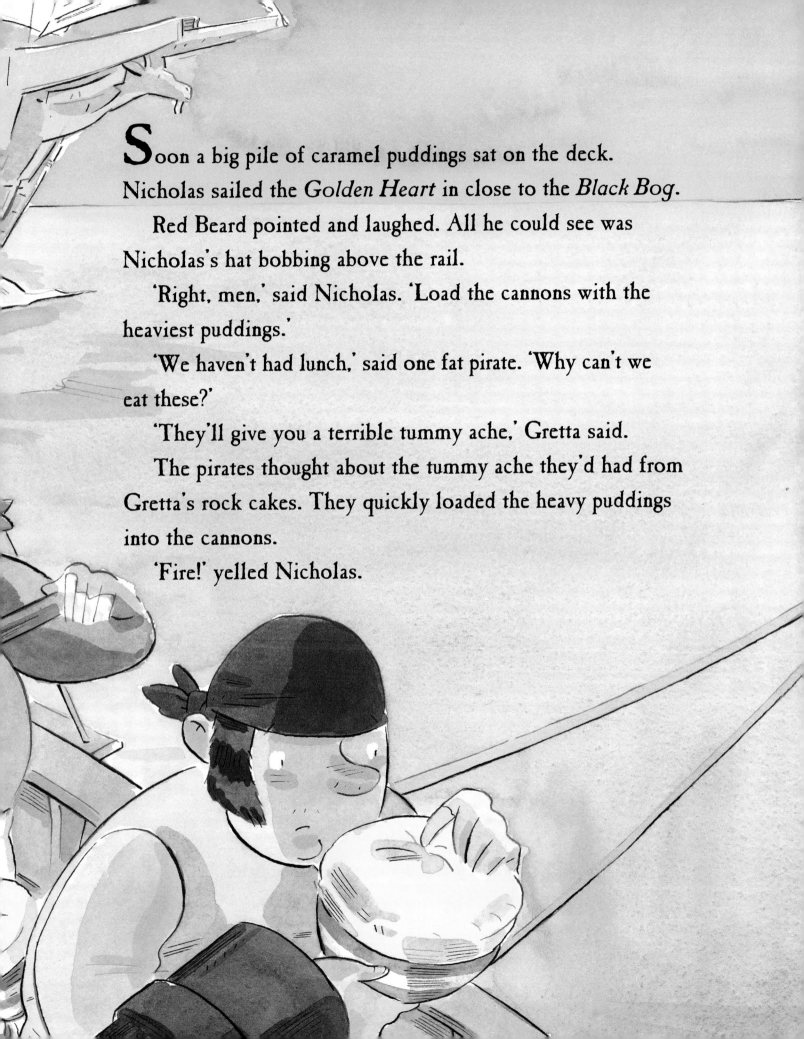

Soon a big pile of caramel puddings sat on the deck. Nicholas sailed the *Golden Heart* in close to the *Black Bog*.

Red Beard pointed and laughed. All he could see was Nicholas's hat bobbing above the rail.

'Right, men,' said Nicholas. 'Load the cannons with the heaviest puddings.'

'We haven't had lunch,' said one fat pirate. 'Why can't we eat these?'

'They'll give you a terrible tummy ache,' Gretta said.

The pirates thought about the tummy ache they'd had from Gretta's rock cakes. They quickly loaded the heavy puddings into the cannons.

'Fire!' yelled Nicholas.

One after the other, puddings sailed through the air and hit the *Black Bog*. Two masts broke with loud cracks.

'Load the runny puddings!' Nicholas shouted. 'Fire!'

The runny puddings splattered all over Red Beard's ship. The sails stuck together. The ropes were too slimy to hold. Red Beard's pirates slipped and skidded in the caramel. They couldn't stand up at all.

One pudding hit Red Beard smack in the chest. He fell over and stuck fast to the deck. Caramel dripped off his hat. The spiders leapt out of his beard and ran away.

Nicholas took his axe, grabbed a rope and swung across to the *Black Bog*. His pirates followed, scrambling over the rails.

'Look out, you yellow-livered leeks!' they yelled.

'Surrender, you soggy sacks of sausages!'

Red Beard's pirates tried to fight back. But their cutlasses slid out of their hands and their pistols were clogged with caramel. They were soon rounded up and thrown overboard.

Gretta cheered. The fattest pirates picked up bits of pudding and tasted them.

'Urrgh!' said one. 'Like old leather boots.'

'Bleuck!' said another. 'Like frog slime.'

Nicholas took his axe and cut the ropes to free his family. Then he raced down to the hold and chopped a big hole in the bottom of the *Black Bog*. Water started to rush in.

But while he was below, Red Beard had pulled free of the caramel. He was waiting for Nicholas on deck, his cutlass ready.

As Nicholas climbed the stairs, Red Beard shouted, 'I'll fix you, you little rat!' He stabbed at Nicholas.

But Nicholas was fast as well as little. He dodged and dived and twisted and turned. Then he ducked in and chopped off Red Beard's big toe.

'Oooowwwww!' While Red Beard cried and looked for his toe, Nicholas ordered his pirates off the *Black Bog*. 'It's going down fast,' he said. Then he swung back to the *Golden Heart*, where his family was waiting.

'Well done,' said his dad.

'You were very brave,' said his mum.

His brother and sister didn't say anything.

They were too amazed.

'I'm glad my puddings were useful,' said Gretta. 'I think I'll make chocolate mudcakes next.'

Nicholas gulped. 'What about some nice meat pies for the crew?'

'Yes, please!' shouted the pirates.

As the *Black Bog* sank, the sea gurgled and bubbled.

'It's a pity about the *Black Bog*,' said Dad. 'I need a new ship. Red Beard burned mine.'

'What about this one?' asked Nicholas.

'Oh no,' said Dad. 'The *Golden Heart* is your ship now.'

'Hooray!' said Nicholas. 'Then Gretta is my first mate. And I'm going to call my ship the *Golden Pudding*!'